Three Special Gifts

AF604891

Retold by Carmel Reilly
Illustrations by Sarah DeMonteverde

Contents

Chapter 1

A Clever Plan

Once, long ago, there was a family who lived on a farm in a remote part of China.

The family was made up of an old man, his four adult sons, three daughters-in-law and five grandchildren.

Sadly, the old man's wife had died some years before. This was not only hard for the old man and his sons, but for the three daughters-in-law, too. They really missed having the older woman in the household to help and guide them.

Not having a mother-in-law made the daughters-in-law want to visit their own mothers more often. Because they did not live close to their mothers, they usually only saw them once a year, during the New Year festival.

If they wanted to have extra visits, they had to ask permission from their father-in-law, as he was head of the household. In those days, the head of the household made decisions for the whole family.

Although the old man had allowed his daughters-in-law extra visits before, he did not like them going away. There was a lot of work to do on the farm, and their help was always needed.

It had been some months since the daughters-in-law had seen their mothers. The old man knew they would ask him for a visit soon.

He had thought for a long time about how he could stop them going away so often. If he simply said no, they would become upset with him. He realised that he had to do something that would put an end to the extra visits, without making him seem unkind.

So, when his daughters-in-law came to see him, the old man had a clever plan that he was ready to put into action.

"You can visit your mothers," the old man told them, "but in return you must each bring me back a special gift."

He turned to his first daughter-in-law, who was the oldest, and said, "I want you to bring me the gift of fire in paper."

To the second daughter-in-law, he said, "You must bring me wind in paper."

Then, to the third daughter-in-law, he said, "And from you, I want music in wind."

"How can we get these things?" the three women asked.

"You must work that out yourselves," the old man replied. "But if you fail to bring them to me, you will not be able to visit your mothers again."

Chapter 2

Help from a Stranger

The next day, the daughters-in-law set off together to visit their mothers. They were unusually silent as each of them thought about the gift they needed to bring home.

After a while, the third daughter-in-law stumbled and almost fell.

"My shoe is broken!" she exclaimed. She sat down, took off the shoe and started to cry.

The first daughter-in-law crouched beside her. "Don't cry, I'm sure we can fix your shoe."

"I'm not crying about my shoe," replied the third daughter-in-law. "I'm worried about getting the gifts our father-in-law wants."

Just then, a young woman came along riding a buffalo.

"Are you all right?" she asked, seeing the third daughter-in-law's tears.

"My shoe is broken, and we have a long way to walk!" replied the third daughter-in-law, who didn't want to explain her real troubles to a stranger.

The young woman looked at the shoe. "I live nearby. Come with me and I'll fix it."

The daughters-in-law followed the young woman to a house overlooking green fields. They sat and talked with her while she repaired the shoe.

Soon, the shoe was fixed.

"Oh, thank you!" said the third daughter-in-law, who suddenly began sobbing again.

"What is wrong?" asked the young woman.

The daughters-in-law were silent for a moment.

Then, the second daughter-in-law said, "We have been given impossible tasks by our father-in-law. That is what is troubling her."

"What are the tasks?" asked the young woman.

After they told her, she thought for a moment and said, "I can help you with that, too. Come here on your way home next week."

Chapter 3

A Great Surprise

After a happy week visiting their mothers, the daughters-in-law set off back to the farm. On the way, they stopped by the young woman's house.

"I have your gifts ready," the young woman said. She gave the first daughter-in-law a paper lantern with a candle inside. Then, she passed a paper fan to the second daughter-in-law, and wind chimes to the third.

As the daughters-in-law looked at the gifts, the young woman explained what they were.

"You are so clever!" cried the first daughter-in-law. "These are exactly what Father-in-law has asked for!"

As soon as they returned home, the three women rushed to see their father-in-law.

The first daughter-in-law lit the candle inside the paper lantern and handed it to him. "Here is the gift you asked for. It is fire in paper," she said.

The old man's eyes grew wide.

The second daughter-in-law stepped forward and waved the paper fan through the air. "Here is my gift to you. It is wind in paper."

At this, the old man started to turn pale.

Finally, the third daughter-in-law approached. "Here is my gift of music in wind!" she said, holding the wind chimes up to the breeze.

The old man's mouth dropped open.

"How did you know what to bring me?" he asked, shocked that they had done what he had thought they never would.

"We met a clever young woman on our journey," said the first daughter-in-law. "She was the one who worked out what you wanted."

The old man looked very interested. "Tell me about her," he said.

Chapter 4

A New Daughter-in-Law

The old man knew straight away that this young woman was very clever. He decided that she would make a wonderful fourth daughter-in-law.

In those days, all marriages first had to be agreed to by the families. After talking to the young woman's family, the old man was able to arrange a marriage between the young woman and his last unmarried son.

The wedding took place soon after, and the young woman moved to the family's farm.

The three daughters-in-law loved their new sister-in-law, as she was so kind and clever. She was also hard-working, and quickly helped to improve the farm.

The old man, who was growing tired, was so pleased with her that he soon made her the head of the household.

The young woman's first decision as head of the household was to buy a buffalo to plough the fields. This meant less work for the family, giving them more spare time.

Her second decision was to allow the daughters-in-law to visit their mothers whenever they wished.

Everyone in the family was very happy. The farm was in good hands.